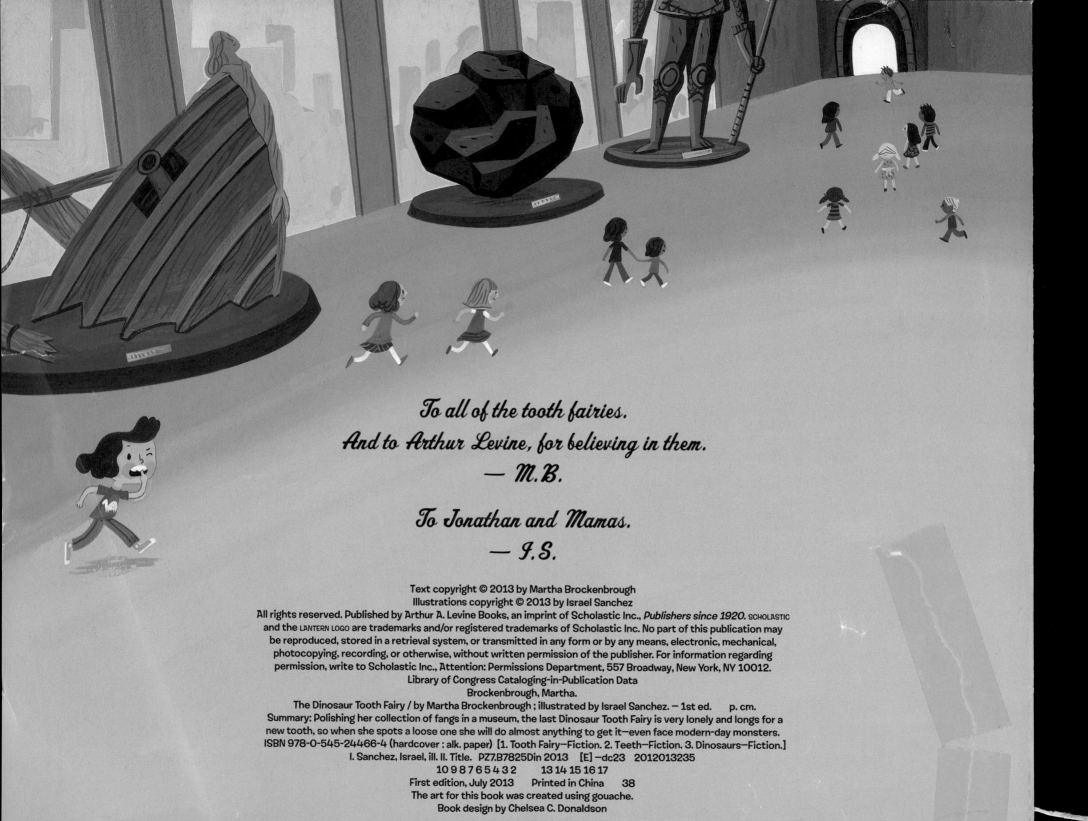

To all of the tooth fairies.
And to Arthur Levine, for believing in them.
— M.B.

To Jonathan and Mamas.
— J.S.

Text copyright © 2013 by Martha Brockenbrough
Illustrations copyright © 2013 by Israel Sanchez
All rights reserved. Published by Arthur A. Levine Books, an imprint of Scholastic Inc., *Publishers since 1920*. SCHOLASTIC
and the LANTERN LOGO are trademarks and/or registered trademarks of Scholastic Inc. No part of this publication may
be reproduced, stored in a retrieval system, or transmitted in any form or by any means, electronic, mechanical,
photocopying, recording, or otherwise, without written permission of the publisher. For information regarding
permission, write to Scholastic Inc., Attention: Permissions Department, 557 Broadway, New York, NY 10012.
Library of Congress Cataloging-in-Publication Data
Brockenbrough, Martha.
The Dinosaur Tooth Fairy / by Martha Brockenbrough ; illustrated by Israel Sanchez. — 1st ed.   p. cm.
Summary: Polishing her collection of fangs in a museum, the last Dinosaur Tooth Fairy is very lonely and longs for a
new tooth, so when she spots a loose one she will do almost anything to get it—even face modern-day monsters.
ISBN 978-0-545-24466-4 (hardcover : alk. paper) [1. Tooth Fairy—Fiction. 2. Teeth—Fiction. 3. Dinosaurs—Fiction.]
I. Sanchez, Israel, ill. II. Title. PZ7.B7825Din 2013   [E] —dc23   2012013235
10 9 8 7 6 5 4 3 2   13 14 15 16 17
First edition, July 2013   Printed in China   38
The art for this book was created using gouache.
Book design by Chelsea C. Donaldson

The
DINOSAUR
TOOTH
FAIRY

by **Martha Brockenbrough** · illustrated by **Israel Sanchez**

Arthur A. Levine Books
An Imprint of Scholastic Inc.

*I*nside the museum of truly old things, past the food court,

the woolly mammoths, and the wheel exhibit,

the last Dinosaur Tooth Fairy polishes her collection of fangs.

She has a spiky beauty from a Spinosaurus,

a mighty molar from the Gigantosaurus,

and a splendid side tooth she snagged from a yawning duck-billed Hadrosaur.

Those were good days for a Dinosaur Tooth Fairy.

The world was hot, the teeth were huge,

and the tiny dinies made her happy.

But so much time has passed.

And now, the Dinosaur Tooth Fairy

is alone, alone, **alone.**

She knows just what she needs to feel better, though.

A new tooth . . .

Like that one, over there!

It's a teeny-tiny, white, T-riffic doozy of a tooth,

and it's looser than loose. Look!

PLIK!

The Dinosaur Tooth Fairy wants it, wants it, **wants it.**

So she leaves behind her collection of fangs and

tiptoes after the child . . .

. . . who gets swallowed by a giant, roaring monster.

The Dinosaur Tooth Fairy rushes to save the day,

but the monster only blinks his swoopy lashes

and zooms away.

She hangs on tight until at last he stops and coughs

and *fwoosh!* out pops the child.

The Dinosaur Tooth Fairy wants a rest,

but she needs, **needs**, **needs** that tooth.

And so, until the sun goes down, she battles the

one-eyed doorknobosaurus,

who is fierce and impossible.

But at last she defeats him

and lands *plonk!* next to a beast who has splendid

fangs of his own and a great deal of drool.

The doggie's tickled to see her in this house full of teeth,

where some are attached, and some are not.

Yet there's still just the one thing she wants and it's nowhere,

nowhere, nowhere to be found. She tries one last spot . . .

but the tooth isn't in the shirt cave.

Nor is it with the small furry mammal.

It's definitely not with the parrot,

who is rude, **rude**, **rude** and that is ALL there is to say.

And now the sun is rising and she doesn't have what she wants and this is terrible, terrible, terrible.

Just as she's about to give up, she hears

the child and sniffs the air —

IT'S THE TOOTH!

Over the bed, but under the pillow,

which is a problem, because her arms are as short

as her tantrums are long.

Is that the sound of a heart breaking?

It's not, it's not, it's not.

It's the sound of two new friends who've found the teeth of their dreams,

and something else they love even more.